William D. Malto.

The Duties of Covering Serjeants in Company and Battalion Drill

SALZWASSER
VERLAG

William D. Malton

The Duties of Covering Serjeants in Company and Battalion Drill

Reprint of the original, first published in 1859.

1st Edition 2022 | ISBN: 978-3-37513-240-8

Verlag (Publisher): Salzwasser Verlag GmbH, Zeilweg 44, 60439 Frankfurt, Deutschland
Vertretungsberechtigt (Authorized to represent): E. Roepke, Zeilweg 44, 60439 Frankfurt, Deutschland
Druck (Print): Books on Demand GmbH, In de Tarpen 42, 22848 Norderstedt, Deutschland

THE

DUTIES OF COVERING SERJEANTS

IN

Company and Battalion

DRILL.

IN ACCORDANCE WITH THE REVISED FIELD EXERCISE.

BY

WILLIAM D. MALTON, M.A.,

LATE 2ND ROYAL MIDDLESEX RIFLES.

(Author of " Company and Battalion Drill Illustrated.")

LONDON:

PRINTED AND PUBLISHED BY

W. CLOWES AND SONS, 14, CHARING CROSS.

1859.

PREFACE.

THE following directions for Covering Serjeants have been compiled from *Company and Battalion Drill Illustrated,* in compliance with numerous suggestions made to the Author by Officers in possession of that work.

June 1859.

☞ The marginal words of command (printed in CAPITALS) are those given by the Drill Instructor in PART I, and by the Battalion Commander in PART II.

In PART II. the Major's words are distinguished by smaller capitals: thus—STEADY.

The reference F. E. is to the *Field Exercise*, 1859.

INTRODUCTION.

(1) *Degrees of March.*

In *Slow* or *Quick* time the length of a pace is 30 inches: except in " stepping out," when it is 33 inches, and in " stepping short," when it is 10 inches.

> [In *Wheeling* (forward or backward): the outer man, only, of the Company takes a full pace; each of the other men shortening his pace in proportion to his distance from the standing flank.]

In *Double* time (in which there is neither ' stepping out' nor ' stepping short') the length of a pace is 36 inches.

The length of the *Side-step*, which is always taken in quick time, is 10 inches: except when taken to clear or cover another man (as in forming four-deep), in which case it will be 21 inches.

In Slow time   75 steps (=62 yds. 18 in.)⎫
In Quick time 108   „   (=90 yards)   ⎬ are taken in a
In Double time 150   „   (=150 yards)   ⎭ minute.

The command for " marking time " from the Halt is *Mark-time: Quick* (or *Slow*).   (F. E. I., pp. 12, 13.)

(2) *To calculate paces for Files.*

Multiply the number of files by 7, and cut off the right-hand figure of the result.

N.B.—If a Company wheels the same number of paces that it contains files, it will wheel the Quarter circle: if it wheels half that number of paces, it will complete the eighth of a circle: if a quarter of the number, it will complete the sixteenth of a circle. (*See* Fig I., p. 54.)

(3) *Meaning of the terms "Proper pivot," " Inner," and "Outer,"*
    flank.

The *proper pivot* flank in all single Columns is that which
when wheeled up to, preserves the several parts of a Company
or Line in their natural order, and to their proper front.
Thus: in a Column of Companies *Right in front (i.e.* with
that Company leading which when in Line stands on the right)
the front-rank *left-*hand man of each Company is the pivot on
which if a wheel into Line were made, the Line would stand in
its proper order.   Similarly: in a Column *Left in front (i.e.*
with that Company leading which when in Line stands on the
left) the front-rank *right-*hand men of Companies are the
pivots.

Hence the expression, " Right in front : Left the pivot," and
vice versâ.

The flank opposite to the pivot is called the *Reverse* flank.

[The above explanation equally applies to a single Column of Subdivisions or Sections.]

The term 'Inner' flank is applied to the pivot flank in
Column, to the flank next to the preceding Company in *Echellon,*
and to the flank nearest the point of *appui* in *Line:* the opposite
is called the ' Outer' flank.

(4) *How to size a Company.*

A Company is sized from flanks to centre, as follows—

The men are first formed in a single rank; the tallest
on the flanks, the shortest in the centre.   Each Subdivision is
then formed two-deep: the left files of the Right Subdivision
forming in rear, those of the Left Subdivision in front, of the
right files.   [The left-hand man of the Company, if a right
file, will also take a pace to the front.]   The whole are then
closed and dressed on the right file.

Odd numbers are right files, even numbers left files. Should the file on the left of the Company, however, be an odd number, it will act as a left file: and the left-but-one file—although an even number—will act as a right file. If there is a *blank* file (*i.e.* a file without a rear-rank man), it must be the 3rd file from the left of the Company.

Should there be an uneven number of files in the Company, one Subdivision must, of course, be stronger than the other. When this is the case in a *Right* Company (*i.e.* one whose number, as it stands in the Battalion, is odd), the odd file will be included in the Right Subdivision: in a *Left* Company (*i.e.* one whose number in the Battalion is even), the odd file will be in the Left Subdivision. When the 2 Sections of *either* Subdivision are unequal, the stronger of the two will be that on the outer flank. (F. E., pp. 48, 49.)

(5) *Wheeling on 'fixed' and 'moveable' pivots.*

A wheel is said to be made on a 'fixed (or halted) pivot' when—the Company being at the Halt—the pivot-man on the *Caution, faces* into the named direction: on a 'moveable pivot,' when—the Company being on the move—the pivot-man brings his inner shoulder gradually round with the rest of the Company, at the same time circling round the wheeling point with very short paces.

A wheel may also be made on a 'moveable pivot from the Halt.' In this case the *Caution* will commence with the words ON THE MOVE: and the pivot-man, instead of facing, will circle round (as when on the march) into the new direction; the Company getting the word FORWARD when the required degree of wheel is completed.

The following *General Rules* are equally applicable to a Company formed singly, or with the Battalion:—

I. On all occasions when a Company, Subdivision, or Section wheels *forward*, the rear-rank man of the pivot file

will uncover by taking a pace to his rear, and then a side-step
of 21 inches, so as to cover the rear-rank man of the file next
him: but when the wheel is made *backwards*—whether the
men are faced-about to wheel, or not—he will not uncover.

[The front-rank man of the pivot file is usually termed
"the pivot man."]

(F. E., p. 54.)

II. When the word *Quick*, or *Double March* is given to
men standing with carried Arms, they will (*except when
wheeling on a standing pivot* slope—or, if *Riflemen*, will trail—
as they step off: during the Slow, Side, or Back step, they remain at the carry, unless ordered to slope or trail.

The men will invariably carry from the slope when they
halt.

If Arms are at the order when *Slow* or *Quick March* is
given, the men trail: and men marching at the trail when
Halt is given, order. In turning about: Arms are carried
from the slope (or brought to a perpendicular position from the
trail), on the first pace: the original position being resumed as
the men, on the 4th pace, step off in the new direction. When
men standing with ordered Arms are directed to close, to step
back, or to take any named number of paces to the front,
they will come to the short trail: ordering as they halt.

F. E., p. 5.

In Part I the cases in which a Corering giving a point *penalises*, and
carries his Arms, are mentioned as they occur: in Part II a general rule is
given.

POSTING OF COVERING SERJEANTS.

Covering Serjeants are posted—

(1) *In a Company in Line at Close order:*
   On the right of the rear rank.

(2) *In Column of Companies:*
   One pace in rear of the 2nd file from the pivot flank.

(3) *In Column of Subdivisions or Sections:*
   One pace in rear of the 2nd file of the leading Subdivision or Section.

   [In Column of Sections, if there is no Supernumerary Serjeant to lead the 2nd Section, it will be led by the Coverer.]

(4) *In File-marching, and the flank march by Fours:*
   The Coverer marches at the head of the front rank.

   Exception. When a *close* Column takes ground to a flank by Fours, the Coverer of each Company (if on the leading flank) marches at the head of the 2nd rank; the Captain leading the front rank.

(5) *In Echellon (Oblique or Direct) of Companies:*
   The Coverer of each Company is on the reverse flank of its front rank.

   [In Echellon of Subdivisions or Sections, the Coverer retains his position.]

When the Captain changes his flank, the Coverer (except when required to take a point, or when the Company is closing) will change with him: passing, on all occasions, by the *rear*. [When both the Captain and Coverer change by the rear, the latter will always *follow* the former.]

A Coverer, both in moving out to give a point and in changing his flank, will move in Double time.

Part I.—COMPANY DRILL.

N.B.—A Company will always be drilled as though it were with the Battalion. The Drill Instructor will state, previously to each movement, the supposed formation of the Battalion, thus— AS A COMPANY IN LINE, or AS A COMPANY IN COLUMN RIGHT (or LEFT) IN FRONT: and the Coverer (if not already in his place) will take post accordingly.

No. 1. *When a Company as in Line takes Open order, and resumes Close order.*

(F. E., p. 55.)

REAR RANK TAKE OPEN ORDER.

MARCH.

(1) *On the word* ORDER—The Coverer takes a side step of 21 inches to his left, into the place vacated by the right-hand man of the rear rank.

(2) *On the word* MARCH—He takes one pace to his right with the right foot, and one pace to his front with the left foot into the Captain's place.

REAR RANK TAKE CLOSE ORDER.

MARCH.

On the word MARCH—The Coverer takes 2 paces to his rear, and one pace to his left: and when the supernumerary Officers have passed to the rear, moves up to his place on the right of the rear rank.

No. 2. *When a Company as in Column (Right in front) marching in Slow time, takes Open order, and resumes Close order.*

(F. E., p. 58.)

COMPANY: BY
THE RIGHT.

REAR RANK
TAKE OPEN
ORDER.

(1) *On the word* RIGHT—The Coverer changes his flank.

(2) *On the word* ORDER—He moves up into the place vacated by the Captain, and leads the Company.

On the *Caution* to take CLOSE ORDER, the Coverer falls back to the rear of the 2nd file from the pivot flank.

No. 3. *When a Company as in Column wheels into Line.*

(F. E., pp. 59, 69.)

LEFT (*or*
RIGHT)WHEEL
INTO LINE.

Q. MARCH.

(A.) *From the Halt.*

(1) *On the word* LINE —The Coverer runs to the front, and marks the spot where the wheeling flank of the Company will rest when the wheel is completed: standing (with shouldered Arms) facing in the direction of the new front; raising his left arm from the elbow; and looking towards, and aligning himself with, the pivot man.

(2) *At the Captain's word* " *Eyes front* "— The Coverer falls back to his place on the right of the rear rank.

LEFT (*or*
RIGHT)
WHEEL INTO
LINE.

FORWARD.

(B.) *On the March.*

The Coverer, if Right is in front, moves across: if Left is in front, moves up: to his proper post in Line, during the wheel.

[When a Company in Line *retires*, the Coverer remains in his place in the *proper* rear rank.]

No. 4. *When a Company as in Line wheels into Column.*

(F. E. pp. 61, 69.)

OPEN COLUMN,
RIGHT (*or*
LEFT) IN
FRONT.
___
RIGHT-ABOUT
FACE.
___
RIGHT (*or*
LEFT) WHEEL:
___
Q. MARCH.

(A.) *From the Halt.*

(1) *On the word* FRONT—The Coverer runs to the rear, and marks the spot where the wheeling flank of the Company will rest when the wheel is completed: standing (with shouldered Arms) facing in the direction that the Column will face; and raising his left arm.

(2) *At the Captain's word " Halt, front: dress"*—The Coverer falls into his proper place in Column.

COMPANY:
RIGHT (*or*
LEFT) WHEEL.
___
FORWARD.

(B.) *On the March.*

The Coverer, if the wheel is to the right, moves across: if the wheel is to the left, falls back: into his place in Column, during the wheel.

[The same directions apply if the Movement is done from the Halt, ON THE MOVE.]

No. 5. *When a Company as in Line or Column wheels any given number of paces on either flank, from the Halt.*

(F. E., p. 62.)

— PACES
RIGHT (*or*
LEFT) WHEEL.
or
— PACES ON
THE RIGHT (*or*
LEFT) BACK-
WARDS
WHEEL.
___
Q. MARCH.

(1) *On the word* WHEEL—The Coverer will place himself with his back to the 8th file from the pivot, in front or rear of that file according as the wheel is to be made forward or backward: and having taken the named number of paces along the circumference of the circle of which the pivot is the

centre (*see* Plate), will halt [or, if he has taken the paces to the *rear*, will halt and front].

(2) *On the Captain's word " Eyes front "* — The Coverer will return to the place he occupied previous to the *Caution.*

N.B.—The 8th file wheeling 8 paces will complete the Quarter circle: 4 paces, the eighth of a circle: 2 paces, the sixteenth of a circle. (*See* FIG. II., p. 54.)

No. 6. *When a Company as in Line or Column wheels on the Centre, from the Halt.*

(F. E., p. 63.)

[The word WHEEL, given at the *Halt*, always implies the Quarter circle.]

ON THE
CENTRE,
RIGHT (or
LEFT) WHEEL.

Q. MARCH.

(1) *On the word* WHEEL—The Coverer will move out, and align himself with the pivot man, with shouldered Arms; marking the spot where the outer flank of the wheeling-forward Subdivision will rest. [This flank will, in most cases, become the pivot.]

(2) *At the Captain's word " Dress " [or "Eyes front "]*—The Coverer falls into his place in Line or Column as the case may be.

[The left-hand man of the Right Subdivision is always considered the centre of the Company.]

N.B.—In wheeling on the Centre:—A Company as in Line if wheeled to the right, becomes a Company as in Column Right in front: if wheeled to the left, becomes a Company as in Column Left in front. Similarly—a Company as in Column

Right in front, if wheeled to the left; and a Company as in Column Left in front, if wheeled to the right; will wheel into *Line.*

When a Company as in Line is required to wheel on its Centre any given number of paces (less than the Quarter circle) *as if preparatory to a change of front in Line* [*see* No. 27 of PART II.]:—the Coverer will step his paces from the 8th file from the *centre*, counting towards the outer flank of the wheeling-forward Subdivision.

No. 7. *Wheeling forward by Subdivisions (or Sections) from Line.*

(F. E. pp., 65, 69.)

(A.) *From the Halt.*

BY SUBDI-
VISIONS [*or*
SECTIONS]:
RIGHT (*or*
LEFT) WHEEL.
Q. MARCH.

At the Captain's word " *Halt, dress* "—The Coverer will take his proper place in Column.

[When the wheel is to be BACKWARDS:—on the word WHEEL, the Coverer will move back, and mark (with shouldered Arms) the spot where the wheeling flank of the future leading Subdivision (or Section) will rest in Column: taking post in Column (as usual) at the Captain's word *Halt, dress.*]

(B.) *On the March.*

SUBDIVISIONS
[*or* SECTIONS]:
RIGHT (*or*
LEFT) WHEEL.
FORWARD.

The Coverer, when the wheel is to the right, will move across to his place in Column during the wheel: when the wheel is to the left, he will

..... his Captain when the latter doubles up to
.. .. Subdivision (or Section).

.. the *Echellon March* of Subdivisions (or
.......) the Coverer retains the place he occupied
........ly to the wheel into Echellon.]

---

*When an Open Column of Subdivisions (or
Sections) wheels into Line.*

(F. E., pp. 67, 69.)

(A.) *From the Halt.*

(.. the *word* LINE—The Coverer will move out to
mark the spot where the wheeling flank of the
leading Subdivision (or Section) of the Column
will rest in Line: with shouldered Arms, and the
left arm raised.

(.) *On the Captain's word "Eyes front"*—The
Coverer will take his proper place in Line.

(B.) *On the March.*

The Coverer, if Right is in front, will move to his
place in Line by the rear: if Left is in front, round
the reverse flank(s) of the rear Subdivision (or
Sections): during the wheel.

No. 9. *When a Company in Column of Subdivisions
(or Sections) forms to the reverse flank.*

(F. E., p. 73.)

(1) *When the leading Subdivision (or Section) is
halted*—The Coverer runs out to mark the spot
where the reverse flank of the Company will rest

in Line: facing towards the pivot flank, and *recovering* his Arms.

(2) *At the Captain's word " Eyes front,"* the Coverer falls into his place in Line.

No. 10. *Formations from File or Fours.*

(F. E., pp. 74—76.)

FRONT FORM
COMPANY
[SUBDIVISIONS
or SECTIONS].
———
FORWARD.

(1) *Forming to the Front.*

The Coverer moves across to his place (by the rear) during the formation : or, if *Subdivisions* or *Sections* are formed, at the word FORWARD.

ON THE LEAD-
ING FILE:
RIGHT (or
LEFT) FORM
COMPANY.

(2) *Forming Company to the Reverse flank.*

The Coverer marks the outward flank of the Company, facing (with recovered Arms) to the pivot flank, from which the Captain will dress the men: and at the word " *Eyes front* " falls into his place.

ON THE LEAD-
ING FILE:
RIGHT- (or
LEFT-)
ABOUT FORM
COMPANY.

(3) *Forming Company to the Right- or Left-about.*

The Coverer places himself on the inner flank of the Company, facing (with shouldered Arms) to the new front. He falls in, as usual, at the word "*Eyes front.*"

No. 11. *The Side (or Closing) Step.*

(F. E., p. 76.)

RIGHT (or
LEFT) CLOSE.
———
Q. MARCH.

If (the number of paces not being named) the Captain moves out in front of the Company, the Coverer

C

steps up into his place, and occupies it till his return.

No. 12. *Countermarching by Ranks and Files.*

(F. E., p. 77.)

COUNTER-
MARCH BY
RANKS,
RIGHT AND
LEFT FACE.
——
Q. MARCH.
or
COUNTER-
MARCH BY
FILES. TO
THE — FACE.
— COUNTER-
MARCH.
——
Q. MARCH.

(1) *On the word* RANKS *or* FILES—The Coverer will step up and cover the Captain.

(2) *On the word* FACE—He faces to the right-about.

(3) *On the Captain's word "Dress"*—He drops back to his place in rear.

N.B—In countermarching by Ranks, the men countermarch to the Right: in countermarching by Files, always round the front rank. In the countermarch by Files:—the Company will always be faced *from*, and marched *up to*, the future pivot flank.

No. 13. *A Company diminishing Front by forming Subdivisions: and Subdivisions forming Sections.*

(F. E., pp. 78—81.)

FORM SUB-
DIVISIONS.
——
(*Suppose Right
in front*)
LEFT SUB-
DIVISION :
RIGHT-ABOUT
THREE
QUARTERS
FACE.
——
Q. MARCH.

N.B.—In diminishing the front of a Company (or Column of Subdivisions) the *pivot* Subdivision (or Sections) will double in rear of the *reverse*.

Whether this movement is done from the Halt or on the March:—The Coverer moves across with the Captain to the pivot Subdivision (or Section) as soon as it is cleared by that which is doubling in its rear.

No. 14. *Sections increasing Front by forming Sub-divisions: and Subdivisions forming Company.*

(F. E., pp. 81—83.)

FORM SUBDI-VISIONS.

(Suppose Right in front)
LEFT SECTIONS: LEFT HALF FACE.

Q. MARCH.

(A.) *From the Halt.*

Suppose Sections forming Subdivisions—

(1) *On the word* SUBDIVISIONS—The Coverer moves out to mark where the outer flank of the front Sub-division will rest.

(2) *On the Captain's word* " *Dress* "—He takes his proper place in Column.

(B.) *On the March.*

The Coverer moves to his place in rear of the 2nd file from the pivot of the front Subdivision, at the Captain's word " *Front turn.*"

If the Front of a Company as in Column, or of a Column of Subdivisions, is diminished *by breaking off Files*, the Coverer will move up and cover the Captain till *all* the files are again brought up.

No. 15. *Forming Close Column of Sections, and Company Square.*

(F. E., p. 84.)

[The Column is formed on the 2nd Section.]

FORM CLOSE COLUMN OF SECTIONS. Q. MARCH.

PREPARE FOR CAVALRY.

The Coverer leads the front rank of the 1st Section into Column: and then covers his Captain.

At the word CAVALRY—He moves into the centre of the Column.

c 2

Re-forming Company.

On the word COLUMN—The Coverer covers the Captain, who will have resumed his place on the flank.

On the word MARCH—He leads the front rank of the 1st Section : and the Company having been formed, falls back to his proper post.

No. 16. *Rallying Square.*

(F. E., p. 86.)

Re-form Company (Subdivision, or Section.)

When a Rallying Square is to be reduced :—On the Captain's word " *Re-form Company (Subdivision, or Section),*" the Coverer marks the pivot flank of the Company, facing the supposed enemy ; and the men form upon him.

END OF COMPANY DRILL.

Part II.—BATTALION DRILL.

General Rules.

1. When the Captain of a Company changes his flank, the Coverer (unless required to take a point) will change with him: passing, on all occasions, by the Rear.

2. Whenever the Captain moves from the front rank (except for the purpose of changing his flank), the Coverer will take his place and preserve it till his return. [When both the Captain and Coverer move out during a formation in Line, the rear-rank man of the pivot file will move up into the Captain's place.]

3. Coverers, when marking points, will stand with recovered Arms, facing towards the 'point of *appui*' (*see* next page): their inner arms marking the alignment. This rule, however, does not apply to the Coverer marking the outer flank of a Company (Subdivision or Section) when wheeling into Line or Column: who will stand with *shouldered* Arms, and his left arm raised, facing towards the new front.

(F. E., pp. 54, 92, 95.)

---

§ *Alignment and Points of Formation.*

An *alignment* is the imaginary straight line between any 2 points, determined previously to a formation, and marked by the Battalion *aides.* That extremity of the alignment on which a formation is made, and *from* which all intermediate points are dressed, is called the ' Point of *Appui*' : the opposite extremity of the alignment, *upon* which the Line or intermediate points are dressed, is termed the ' Distant Point.'

(*a*) On all occasions of the formation of *Line* on a named Company:—The Coverer and senior supernumerary Serjeant of the Company of formation will run out, on the *Caution*, and place themselves opposite each of its flank files, the Coverer taking the flank furthest from the Captain : falling into their places in Line when the formation is completed. The Coverer of each of the other Companies, as it arrives at 20 paces from the new alignment, will run out to mark where its outward flank will rest in Line, covering on the base points of the Company of formation : and (in order that each Coverer may have ·2 points to cover on) will not fall into his place in Line till the 2nd Company from his own gets *Eyes front.*

> The base marked by the 2 Serjeants of the named Company is termed ' the base of Formation'; the points given by the Coverers of the remaining Companies, during the progress of the formation, are called ' intermediate points.'

[The alignment taken up by the *aides,* will be at arms' length from the line of Coverers.]

Coverers giving points always face to the point of *appui.* Thus : if the formation is on the right flank Company, they will face to the Right ; if on the left flank Company, to the Left; if on any central Company, they will face inwards. The dressing and covering of the points will be corrected on the distant *aide* by the Major nearest the point of formation : or by the Senior Major, when the formation is on the centre of the Battalion.

In formations from Subdivisions or Sections, each Coverer takes up distance for his whole Company.

(*b*) In the formation of *Column* from Line on any named Company :—If the formation is on either flank Company, and the named Company is to be the leading one of the Column, its Coverer will give the base point for the Column : placing himself 6 paces in front of, and facing towards, his Captain. [If the named Company is to be the rear one of the Column, its senior supernumerary Serjeant will give the base point, 6 paces in *rear* of the Captain.]

When the formation is on any central Company (whether Right or Left is to be in front), the Coverer of the named Company will mark the future pivot flank of the Company which will form in front of his own ;. covered on his Captain, but facing to the front.

The remaining Coverers run on to take up their covering, as each arrives within 20 paces of the Column. (*See* No. 10.)

N.B.—The following directions do not apply to the Coverer of the Officer on the left of the Line, unless he is specifically mentioned. By 'the Supernumerary Serjeant' is meant the *senior* supernumerary Serjeant.

Sec. I.—Line Movements.

No. 1. *A Battalion in Line taking Open order, and resuming Close order.*

(F. E., p. 104.)

REAR RANK
TAKE OPEN
[CLOSE] ORDER.

The Coverer of each Company acts as directed in No. 1. of Part I.

MARCH.

[During the performance of the *Manual* and *Platoon*, Serjeants in Line remain steady at the 'Shoulder.']

No. 2. *Dressing a Battalion in Line.*

(F. E., p. 107.)

THE
BATTALION
WILL DRESS
BY THE —.

COVERERS:
— PACES TO
THE FRONT.
Q. MARCH.

STEADY.

BATTALION:
Q. MARCH.

STEADY.

(1) *On the Caution*—If the Line is to dress by the Left, all the Coverers change flanks; *preceding* their Captains.

(2) *On the word* MARCH—The Coverers, (including the Coverer of the Officer on the left of the Line) take the named number of paces straight to their front, face to the named flank, and cover. [A Field Officer will then dress them and give STEADY.]

(3) *On the 2nd word* STEADY.—The Coverers resume their places in Line; the Captains making way for them to pass.

THE
BATTALION
WILL
ADVANCE
[or RETIRE]
AND FIRE BY
WINGS.

No. 3. *Advancing and Retiring by Wings.*

(F. E., p. 108.)

No points are given when Line is re-formed on the leading Wing.

SEC. II.—FORMATIONS OF COLUMN FROM LINE.

OPEN COLUMN
RIGHT
(or LEFT)
IN FRONT.

RIGHT ABOUT
FACE.

RIGHT
(or LEFT)
WHEEL.

Q. MARCH.

No. 4. *A Line wheeling into Open Column.*

(F. E., pp. 135—137.)

(A.) *From the Halt.*

The Coverer whose Company will be the leading Company of the Column, acts precisely as in No. 4 of PART I.

The remaining Coverers :—

(1) *On the word* FACE—Face to the right-about.

(2) *On the word* MARCH—Step off in the proper rear of their Companies; halting, fronting, and moving to their proper places in Column, at their Captain's word *Halt, front: dress.*

(B.) *On the March.*

During the Wheel—If the wheel is to the right, each Coverer will move across : if the wheel is to the left, will fall back : to his proper place in Column.

THE BAT-
TALION WILL
MOVE IN
COLUMN OF
COMPANIES
FROM THE
RIGHT (*or*
LEFT) ALONG
THE REAR.

No. 5. *A Battalion moving in Open Column from either flank along the Rear.*

(F. E., p. 138.)

Each Coverer leads the front rank of his Company (as usual) while it is moving by Fours to the rear of the Line : and at the Captain's word *Front turn,* moves to the rear of the 2nd file from the flank on which the Captain is marching.

RIGHT (*or*
LEFT)
COMPANY TO
THE FRONT.
REMAINING
COMPANIES:
ON THE
MOVE,—
WHEEL.

Q. MARCH.

FORWARD.

No. 6. *A Battalion formed in Line advancing from a Flank in Open Column of Companies (Subdivisions or Sections).*

(F. E., p. 139.)

(A.) *Advancing by Companies.*

On the word FRONT—If the advance is from the Right, the Coverer of the named Company changes his flank.

The remaining Coverers :—

> If the advance is from the Right, move across to their places in Column during the 1st wheel : if the advance is from the Left, fall back into those places directly the word MARCH is given.

(B.) *Advancing by Subdivisions (or Sections).*

On the word FRONT—The Coverer of the Company which is to lead the Column, changes with his Captain to the rear of the inner flank of his outer Subdivision (or Section) : and at the word MARCH, moves up to his proper place in Column.

The remaining Coverers move to their places in Column during the 1st wheel.

[When the Movement is done on the March, *all* the Coverers move to their places in Column during the 1st wheel.]

TWO CENTRE
COMPANIES
(SUBDIVISIONS
or SECTIONS)
TO THE
FRONT.
REMAINING
COMPANIES
(SUBDIVISIONS
or SECTIONS):
ON THE
MOVE,
INWARDS
WHEEL.

Q. MARCH.

FORWARD.

No. 7. *A Battalion in Line advancing from the Centre in Double Column of Companies (Subdivisions or Sections).*

(F. E., p. 140)

The proper Left, unless it is otherwise ordered, is always the directing flank in a Double Column.

On the word FRONT—The Coverers of the 2 flank Companies mark the points on which the Companies (Subdivisions or Sections) of their respective Wings will make their 2nd wheel : the Coverer of the right-flank Company making allowance for the distance which the right-centre Company (Subdivision or Section) will have to incline to the left-centre, to fill the space vacated by the Colour party.

During the 1st wheel—The remaining Coverers move to their places in Column.

The Coverers of the 2 flank Companies move to their places, when those Companies (or their outer Subdivisions or Sections) have completed their 2nd wheel.

No. 8. *A Battalion formed in Line retreating from a Flank in Open Column of Companies (Subdivisions or Sections).*

(F. E., p. 143.)

(Suppose the Retreat by *Companies*.)

RETIRE BY COMPANIES (SUBDIVISIONS *or* SECTIONS) FROM THE LEFT IN REAR OF THE RIGHT, [*or* FROM RIGHT IN REAR OF LEFT.]

On the Caution—The Coverer of the flank Company in rear of which the retreat is to be made, will fall back and give a point (at a distance equal to a Company's breadth, and 3 paces) in rear of the next Company's Coverer. On this point the remaining Companies will make their 2nd wheel.

During the 2nd wheel—The remaining Coverers, in succession, change flanks.

The Coverer giving the wheeling point will march off in his place in the proper rear of his Company, when the Captain gives *Q. March.*

If the Movement is done by *Subdivisions* (or *Sections),* the Coverer giving the wheeling point will take distance accordingly.

[When the Retreat is effected by the Companies
facing, or forming Fours, inwards:—the point will
be given close in rear of the Line. The remaining
Coverers will lead their respective Companies (as
usual) while in file or fours: and at their Captain's
word *Rear turn*, will place themselves in the
proper rear of the 2nd file from the new pivot
flank.]

================

No. 9. *A Battalion formed in Line retreating from
both flanks in rear of the Centre, in Double
Column of Companies (Subdivisions or Sections.)*

(F. E., p. 145.)

RETIRE BY
COMPANIES
(SUBDIVISIONS
or SECTIONS)
FROM BOTH
FLANKS IN
REAR OF THE
CENTRE.

(Suppose the Retreat by Subdivisions.)

On the Caution.—The Coverers of the 2 centre Companies fall back and give the points for the 2nd
wheels of the Subdivisions of their respective Wings,
at Subdivision distance and 3 paces from the outward flanks of the 2 centre Subdivisions.

During the 2nd wheel—The remaining Coverers
change flanks.

The Coverers marking the wheeling points will
step off in the proper rear of the 2 centre Subdivisions, when the left-centre Captain gives *Q.
March.*

[If the Movement is done by Companies or
Sections, the Coverers giving the wheeling points
will take distance accordingly.]

No. 10. *A Battalion in Line forming Open, Close, or Quarter-distance Column on any named Company.*

(F. E., p. 147.)

OPEN (CLOSE, or QUARTER-DISTANCE) COLUMN IN REAR [or FRONT] OF No. 1.

REMAINING COMPANIES: FOURS RIGHT.

Q. MARCH.

STEADY.

(A.) In rear or front of the right-flank Company.

(1.) *If Right is to be in front.*

On the Caution—The Coverer of the named Company moves across by the *front*, and places himself 6 paces in front of, and facing towards, his Captain (who will have changed his flank). He will not fall into his place in Column till, the formation being completed, the Senior Major gives STEADY.

On the word RIGHT—The Coverer of No. 2 will step back and mark the spot where the left of his Company will rest in Column : covering on the Captain and Coverer of No. 1. [He will fall back to his place in Column when his Company gets *Halt, front : dress*, from the Captain.]

Each of the other Coverers will place himself (as usual) in front of his leading four.

On the word MARCH—The Companies in Fours step off. Each Coverer in succession when within 20 paces of the pivot flank of the Column, will run out to take covering and distance for his own Company, in rear of the pivot flank of that last formed : falling into his proper place in Column at his Captain's word *Halt, front : dress*.

(2) *If Left is to be in front.*

On the Caution—The *Supernumerary* Serjeant of No. 1. will give the base point, 6 paces in rear of its Captain (who will *not* change his flank): falling into his place in Column when, the formation being completed, the Senior Major gives sᴛᴇᴀᴅʏ.

On the word ʀɪɢʜᴛ—The Coverer of No. 1 will take up his own distance in front of his Captain ; cover on him and the Supernumerary Serjeant, and then face to the right-about ; marking the future pivot flank of No. 2.

The remaining Coverers place themselves (as usual) in front of their leading fours.

On the word ᴍᴀʀᴄʜ—The Companies in Fours step off : each Coverer in succession running on (when within 20 paces of the line of Coverers) to mark the future pivot flank of the Company which will form in front of his own ; covering on the rear base, and then facing to his right-about. Each. Coverer will move to his proper place in rear of his own Company, when the Company for which he is giving a point gets *Halt, front: dress.*

(B.) In front or rear of the left-flank Company.

(1.) *If Right is to be in front.*

— COLUMN IN FRONT [or REAR] OF No.—

REMAINING COMPANIES : FOURS LEFT.

Q. MARCH.

sᴛᴇᴀᴅʏ.

On the Caution—The Coverer of the named Company changes his flank : and the *Supernumerary* Serjeant of that Company marks the base point in rear of the Captain, as in A (2).

The remaining Coverers proceed as in A (2).

(2) *If Left is to be in front.*

On the Caution—The Coverer of the named Company marks the base point in front of his Captain (who will not change his flank), as in A (1).

The remaining Coverers proceed as in A (1).

(C.) On any central Company.

— COLUMN, RIGHT (*or* LEFT) IN FRONT, ON No. —

REMAINING COMPANIES: FOURS INWARDS.

Q. MARCH.

STEADY.

On the Caution—The Coverer of the named Company (whether Right or Left is to be in front) will mark the future pivot flank of the Company which will form, in the Column, in front of his own. He will cover on his Captain, placing himself square with the Line, and will then face to the right-about; standing fast till, the formation being completed, the Senior Major gives STEADY.

The Coverers on the *right* of the named Company, if Right is to be in front, act as in A(2): if Left is to be in front, act as in A(1).

The Coverers on the *left* of the named Company, if Right is to be in front, proceed as in A(1): if Left is to be in front, proceed as in A(2).

(D.) Column on any named Company facing to the rear.

— COLUMN ON No, —. RIGHT (*or* LEFT) IN FRONT, FACING TO THE REAR.

REMAINING COMPANIES: FOURS OUTWARDS.

RIGHT [*or* LEFT] COUNTERMARCH.

Q. MARCH.

STEADY.

On the Caution—The Coverer of the named Company, if *Left* is to be in front, changes his flank. While his Company is being countermarched by Files, he proceeds as in No. 12 of PART I.: during the formation of the Column, he acts as in (C) above.

The remaining Coverers :—

(Suppose the formation on a central Company.)

Lead their Companies (as usual) while in Fours.

(1) If Right is to be in front, the Coverers on the original right of the named Company run on to take up their covering in the Column as directed for the 'remaining Coverers' in A(1): those on the original left of the named Company, as directed for the 'remaining Coverers' in A(2).

(2) If Left is to be in front, the Coverers on the original right of the named Company take up their covering as directed for the 'remaining Coverers' in A(2): those on the original left, as directed for the 're-maining Coverers' in A(1).

When a halted *Double Column* is formed from Line, the Coverer of the left-centre Company will give a base point in front of his Captain. [If the Column is to be formed of *Subdivisions*, the *Super-numerary* Serjeant of each Company will take up covering and distance for its rear Subdivision.]

Sec. III.—Column Movements.

No. 11. *Forming Close or Quarter-distance Column from any more open Column.*

(F. E., p. 116.)

THE COLUMN
WILL CLOSE
TO THE
FRONT [or
REAR].
___
[REMAINING
COMPANIES:
RIGHT-ABOUT
FACE.]
___
Q. MARCH.

(1) *Closing on the front Company.*

On the Caution—The Coverer of the leading Company will give a base point: placing himself 6 paces in front of, and facing towards, his Captain; and covering on the line of Captains. He will resume his place in Column when the Field Officer who is superintending the covering gives READY.

(2) *Closing on the rear Company.*

On the Caution—

The Coverer of the rear Company places himself 6 paces in rear of his Captain: covering, and resuming his place in Column, as directed for the Coverer of the leading Company in [1].

If the closing is on a central Company, no base point will be given.

No. 12. *A Close or Quarter-distance Column opening from the Rear or Front.*

(F. E., p. 118.)

OPEN OUT TO
— DISTANCE
FROM THE
REAR [*or*
FRONT.]

REMAINING
COMPANIES:
[RIGHT-
ABOUT FACE.]
Q. MARCH.

(1) *Opening from the Rear.*

On the Caution—The Coverer of the rear Company proceeds as in No. 11[2]

(2) *Opening from the Front.*

On the Caution—The Coverer of the leading Company proceeds as in No. 11[1].

[On *rough ground :* Each of the other Coverers, in succession, will run out when the Company in his present rear is halted, and (placing himself clear of the flank of the Column) will mark the proper distance for his own Company : falling into his place in Column at his Captain's word *Halt, front : dress.*]

If the opening is from a central Company, no base point will be given.

D

No. 13. *A Close or Quarter-distance Column wheeling on a fixed pivot.*

(F. E., p. 124.)

COLUMN: LEFT
(*or* RIGHT)
WHEEL.
___
Q. (*or* D.)
MARCH.
___
COLUMN:
HALT.

On the Caution—The Coverer of the leading Company runs out to mark where the outward flank of the Column will rest when the wheel is completed: resuming his place in Column at the word COLUMN: HALT.

[When a Column wheels *on the March*, no point is given.]

No. 14. *A Close or Quarter-distance Column counter-marching by the wheel of Subdivisions round the Centre.*

(F. E., p. 127.)

(1) *From the Halt.*

COUNTER-
MARCH BY
SUBDIVISIONS
ROUND THE
CENTRE.
___
(*Suppose Right
in front*)
RIGHT
SUBDIVISIONS:
RIGHT-ABOUT
FACE [*or*
TURN].
___
Q. (*or* D.)
MARCH.
___
HALT: FRONT.
DRESS.
[*or* FRONT
TURN.]

On the Caution—The Coverers of the front and rear Companies will mark the points on which the pivot and reverse Subdivisions, respectively, will wheel: the Coverer of the front Company placing himself in front of the inner file of his reverse Subdivision; the Coverer of the rear Company, in rear of the inner file of his pivot Subdivision; and both facing to the centre of the Column.

They will resume their places in Column, on the word HALT: FRONT: DRESS.

(2) *On the March.*

On the word RIGHT- (*or* LEFT-) ABOUT TURN—The Coverers of the front and rear Companies give their points as in (1): resuming their places in Column at the word FRONT TURN.

No. 15. *Changing the Order of a Column by the successive march of the rear Companies to the Front.*

(F. E., p. 129.)

BY
SUCCESSIVE
COMPANIES :
REAR WING
TO THE FRONT.

Each Coverer steps short while his Company is moving out of the old Column ; taking the Lieutenant's place when that Officer changes his flank at the word *Front turn.*

No. 16. *Changing the Order of an Open, Half, or Quarter distance Column on a Road.*

(F. E., p. 130.)

BY FOURS
FROM THE
LEFT [or
RIGHT]: REAR
WING TO THE
FRONT.

4th [or 1st]
SECTIONS :
INWARDS
WHEEL.
Q. MARCH.

[This movement is used when the space does not admit of the last.]

Each Coverer leads the front rank of his Company (as usual) while it is moving in fours along the flank of the old Column : and at his Captain's word *Front from Company,* moves to his place in rear of the 2nd file from the new pivot (p. 17).

[The front Company of the old Column will get *Front form Company* as soon as its leading four gains the left (or right) of the Road.]

No. 17. *A Column taking ground to a flank in Fours, or by Subdivisions (or Sections.)*

(F. E., p. 131.)

(1) *By Fours.*

TAKE
GROUND TO
THE RIGHT
(or LEFT)
BY FOURS.

If ground is being taken to the reverse flank, *and the Captains are ordered to change flanks,* the Coverers

D 2

FOURS RIGHT
(*or* LEFT.)
or
TAKE
GROUND TO
THE RIGHT
(*or* LEFT) IN
SUBDIVISIONS
[*or* SECTIONS].

SUBDIVISIONS
[*or* SECTIONS]:
RIGHT (*or*
LEFT) WHEEL.

FORWARD.

change with them as usual : otherwise, they remain in their places.

N.B.—When a *Close* Column takes ground to a flank by Fours, the Coverer of each Company (if on its leading flank) marches at the head of the 2nd rank, the Captain leading the front rank.

(2) *By Sections.*

The Coverers retain their usual places.

[The Supernumerary Serjeant of the leading Company will march (as usual) on the pivot flank of the Section he is leading: the remaining Supernumerary Serjeants leading Sections will, *if the Column is at Quarter distance,* march in rear of their Sections.]

Sec. IV.—Formation of Line from Column.

No. 18. *Wheeling into Line from Open Column.*

(F. E., p. 99.)

(A.) *From the Halt.*

LEFT [*or*
RIGHT]
WHEEL INTO
LINE.

STEADY.

Q. MARCH.

On *the word* LINE—The Coverer of the leading Company of the Column runs out to mark the spot where its wheeling flank will rest in Line : standing (with *shouldered* Arms, and the left arm raised) facing the new front, and aligned with the pivot men. [He will fall into his place in Line when his Captain gives *Eyes front.*]

Each of the other Coverers :—

On the word LINE—If Right is in front, places himself on the right of his Company : if Left is in front, stands fast.

On the word MARCH—If Right is in front, wheels with his Company : if Left is in front, moves up to the right of his Company during the wheel, and preserves his Captain's place : falling back, in both cases, to the right of the rear rank when his Captain gives *Eyes front.*

(B.) *On the March.*

Each Coverer if Right is in front, will move across; if Left is in front, will move up; to his place in Line, during the wheel.

No. 19. *Forming Line to the Front from Open Column on any named Company.*

(F. E., p. 152.)

(A.) From the Halt.

(1) *Line on the leading Company.*

(Suppose Right in front.)

On the Caution—All the Coverers (except the Coverer of the leading Company) change flanks.

The Coverer and Supernumerary Serjeant of the leading Company will mark the base points : the former in front of its left, the latter in front of its right, flank : and both facing to the right (the point of *appui: See* page 22). They will move to their places in Line when the Major gives STEADY at the completion of the movement.

FORM LINE ON THE LEADING COMPANY.

(Suppose Right in front.)

REMAINING COMPANIES : FOUR PACES ON THE RIGHT BACKWARDS WHEEL.

Q. MARCH.

FORM LINE : Q. MARCH.

STEADY.

Each of the other Coverers:—

On the word WHEEL—Places himself in rear of, and
with his back to, the 8th file from the right of his
Company; and having taken 4 paces to the rear
(*see* p. 13) along the circumference of the circle
of which the pivot man is the centre, halts and
fronts in line with the pivot man. [The pivot man
will have faced in the direction that the Company
will face at the completion of the wheel.] Each
Coverer, when his Captain (having halted and
dressed his Company) gives *Eyes front*, will fall in
on the left of his front rank. .

On the 2nd word MARCH—The Companies in Echellon
step off: each Coverer, as he arrives within 20
paces of the alignment, running out and covering
(on the base points) at the point where the left
of his Company will rest in Line; and falling into
his place in Line when the 2nd Company from his
own has formed up in Line, been dressed, and got
the word *Eyes front.*

[When the Column is Left in front:—The Coverer
and Supernumerary Serjeant of the leading Company will give the base points: the former in front
of its *right*, the latter in front of its *left*, flank;
and both facing to the *left* (in that case the point
of *appui*). The Coverer of each of the other
Companies will step his 4 paces from the 8th
file from the *left;* and will march (while in
Echellon) on, and will run out to mark, its *right*
flank.]

N.B.—If the Line is to be formed obliquely to the front of
the Column:—The leading Company will first be wheeled back

on its reverse flank into the required direction: and the remainder will then be wheeled back into Echellon; taking, *in addition to the usual 4 paces,* half the number of paces wheeled back by the leading Company. If the leading Company is wheeled *up,* the remaining Coverers will proceed as in No. 20. (*Forming Line to the Reverse flank.*)

(2) *Line on the Rear Company.*

FORM LINE
ON THE REAR
COMPANY.

REMAINING
COMPANIES:
RIGHT-ABOUT
FACE.

(*Suppose Right
in front.*)
FOUR PACES
ON THE RIGHT
BACKWARDS
WHEEL.

Q. MARCH.

FORM LINE:
Q. MARCH.

STEADY.

Each (except the rear) Company, having been faced to the right-about, will be wheeled backwards on its right or left according as Right or Left is in front.

The Coverers proceed as directed in (1).

(3) *Line on any central Company.*

FORM LINE
ON No. —

COMPANIES
IN FRONT:
RIGHT-ABOUT
FACE.

(*Suppose Right
in front.*)
FOUR PACES
ON THE
RIGHT.
BACKWARDS
WHEEL.
Q. MARCH.

FORM LINE :
Q. MARCH.

STEADY.

The Companies in rear of the named Company proceed as in (1): those in front of it, as in (2).

The Coverer and Supernumerary Serjeant giving the base points in front of the named Company, place themselves the former opposite to its left, the latter opposite to its right flank ; and face each other.

They fall into their places (as usual) at the Major's word STEADY at the completion of the formation.

(B.) Line, on the March, on the leading Company.

During the wheel into Echellon—The Coverer of each

FORM LINE ON
THE LEADING
COMPANY.

(except the leading) Company places himself on its outward flank.

(Suppose Right in front.)
REMAINING COMPANIES: LEFT WHEEL.

FORWARD.

The Coverer and Supernumerary Serjeant of the leading Company run out to give the base points (as in the same formation from the Halt), when the Captain of that Company gives *Halt: dress* (*up*).

The remaining Coverers, as they come up, in succession, to 20 paces from the alignment, run out (as usual) to take up their covering in the line of points.

No. 20. *A Battalion in Open Column forming Line to the Reverse flank.*

(F. E., p. 157.)

FORM LINE TO THE REVERSE FLANK.

STEADY.

On the Caution—The Coverer of each Company steps up into the place vacated by his Captain (who will change his flank).

The Coverer and Supernumerary Serjeant of the leading Company, when its Captain gives *Right* (or *Left*) *wheel*, run out to mark the base; both facing towards the Captain, the Coverer taking the flank furthest from him. They will both take post in Line (as usual) at the Major's word **STEADY.**

The Coverer of each of the other Companies will march on its reverse flank (as when in Echellon) till within 20 paces of the alignment, when he will run out, as usual, to take up his covering in the line of Coverers.

[For a Column of *Subdivisions* (or *Sections*) forming Line as above, *see* No. 9, of PART I.]

No. 21. *Forming Line to the front from a Double Column on the March.*

(F. E., p. 159.)

N.B.—In forming Line *to the front* from Double Column:—If the Column is on the March, Line will be formed by Echellon on the same principle as from a Single Column on the March (*see* No. 19 B.): but if the Column is at the Halt it will be closed to Quarter-distance, and then deployed, (*see* No. 23.)

(*On the March.*) FORM LINE ON THE TWO CENTRE SUBDIVISIONS.

REMAINING SUBDIVISIONS: OUTWARDS WHEEL.

FORWARD.

STEADY.

(Suppose a Double Column of Subdivisions on the March.)

The Coverer of each of the 2 centre Companies, when his inner Subdivision is halted, will give a base point where the outward flank of his whole Company will retain Line; facing inwards (*i.e.* to the centre of the Battalion).

They will both take post in Line, as usual, on the Major's word STEADY at the completion of the formation.

[The centre Serjeant will give a centre base point, at arm's length from the centre *aide:* facing to the right.]

The remaining Coverers of each Wing run out (as usual) to take up covering in the line of Coverers: each allowing distance for his whole Company, and covering on the central base points.

No. 22. *A Battalion in Double Column forming Line to the Right or Left.*

(F. E., p. 161.)

(Suppose a Double Column of *Subdivisions*, forming Line to the Right.)

(A.) *On the March.*

FORM LINE
TO THE
RIGHT.

RIGHT WING:
RIGHT WHEEL.

STEADY.

On the word WHEEL—The *Supernumerary* Serjeant of No. 1 marks the right of the intended Line.

Each Coverer of the right Wing immediately runs out to mark where the left of his (whole) Company will rest in Line: facing to the right.

The left-wing Subdivisions will form successively to their reverse flank: the Coverers of that Wing proceeding as in No. 9 of PART I.

[Line will be formed to the LEFT in like manner: the Coverers of the left Wing proceeding as above directed for those of the right Wing: and *vice versâ.*]

FORM LINE
TO THE
RIGHT.

RIGHT WING:
RIGHT WHEEL
INTO LINE.

THE WHOLE:
Q. MARCH.

STEADY.

(B.) *From the Halt.*

The Coverers of the named Wing proceed as in No. 8 of PART I.

The remaining Coverers act as in No. 9 of PART I.

SEC. V.—DEPLOYMENTS.

No. 23. *A Battalion in Close or Quarter-distance Column deploying into Line on any named Company.*

(F. E., pp. 163–168.)

N.B.—Deployments are always made on the base of the front Company.

(Suppose Right in front.)
DEPLOY ON THE LEADING COMPANY.

REMAINING COMPANIES: FOURS LEFT.

Q. MARCH.

STEADY.

(A.) *On the leading Company.*

On the Caution—The Coverer and Supernumerary Serjeant of the leading Company will mark the base points; the former in front of its left, the latter in front of its right, flank: both facing to the right. They will fall into their places in Line (as usual) at the Major's word STEADY at the completion of the formation.

On the word FOURS LEFT—The Coverer of No. 2 will run out to mark the left of his Company, covering on the base points.

Each of the other Coverers leads the front rank of his Company while in fours; and runs out (as usual) when within 20 paces of the alignment, to mark where its outward flank will rest in Line.

> [If the Column is Left in front, the base points face to the *left*: and the Coverers runs out to mark the *right* of their Companies.]

(Suppose Right in front.)
DEPLOY ON THE REAR COMPANY.

REMAINING COMPANIES:

(B.) *On the rear Company.*

On the Caution—The Coverer and Supernumerary Serjeant of the rear Company will move up to the front of the Column, and give the base points close

FOURS RIGHT.

Q. MARCH.

STEADY.

in front of No. 1 : the Coverer placing himself on the right of that Company; the Supernumerary Serjeant on its left; and both facing to the left. They will resume their places (as usual) at the Major's word STEADY.

The remaining Coverers change flanks on the *Caution:* and, during the formation, proceed as in (A).

[If the Column is Left in front, the base points face to the *right;* and the Coverers run out and mark the *left* of their Companies.]

(C.) *On a central Company.*

On the Caution—The Coverer and Supernumerary Serjeant of the named Company give the base points as explained in (B.) : but both facing *inwards.*

DEPLOY ON
No. COMPANY.

REMAINING
COMPANIES:
FOURS OUT-
WARDS.

Q. MARCH.

STEADY.

The Coverers in rear of the named Company proceed as the ' remaining Coverers' in (A.) : those in front of the named Company act as the ' remaining Coverers' in (B).

[The centre *aide* will give a point at arm's length from the Supernumerary Serjeant of the named Company.]

In Deployments from *Double Column,* the centre Serjeant and the Coverers of the 2 centre Companies give base points. [If the Column is one of Subdivisions, the outward flank, only, of each Company will be marked by its Coverer.]

¶ *A Line changing front by the intermediate formation of Open Column on any named Company.*

When front is to be changed to the Right (on whatever Company), the Column will be formed

Left in front, and the named Company—if required to wheel back—will wheel back on its right: when front is to be changed to the Left, *vice versâ*.

The Coverer of the Company of formation will change flank (if necessary), with his Captain.

The remaining Coverers:—During the formation of the Column, proceed as in No. 10.

When the Column is wheeled into Line, all the Coverers act as in No. 18.

N.B.—When the change of front is on a central Company, and the new Line is to be formed *obliquely* to the old:—The Coverer of the named Company will give the new direction; marking the covering and distance for the Company which will form in front of his own in the Column; and being dressed, by a mounted Officer, on the new alignment.

(F. E., p. 169.)

Sec. VI. Echellon Movements.

No. 24. *A Battalion wheeling forward into Echellon.*

(F. E., p. 188.)

(A.) *From the Halt, on fixed pivots.*

WHEEL INTO ECHELLON OF COMPANIES TO THE RIGHT (or LEFT.)

On the Caution—Coverers change flanks if necessary.

COMPANIES:— PACES RIGHT (or LEFT) WHEEL.

On the word WHEEL—The Coverer of each Company places himself in front of the 8th file from its named flank, takes the ordered number of paces to the front, and stands fast till his Captain gives *Eyes front.*

Q. MARCH.

(*See* p. 13.) He then falls in on the reverse flank of his front rank, his proper post in Echellon.

N.B.—An Echellon of *Subdivisions* (or *Sections*) will not be formed on fixed pivots.

TAKE GROUND TO THE RIGHT (*or* LEFT) IN ECHELLON OF COMPANIES [SUBDIVISIONS *or* SECTIONS.]

ON THE MOVE, BY COMPANIES, &c. RIGHT (*or* LEFT) WHEEL.

FORWARD.

(B.) *On moveable pivots.*

On the word FORWARD——If the Echellon is formed of *Companies*, each Coverer falls in on the reverse flank of his Company : if the Echellon is formed of *Subdivisions* or *Sections*, he remains in his place.

No. 25. *A Battalion in Oblique Echellon of Companies re-forming Line.*

(F. E., p. 191.)

(A.) *Line parallel to the original Line.*

WHEEL BACK INTO LINE.

Q. MARCH.

(From the Halt.)

On the Caution—Each Coverer if not already on the right of his Company, changes to that flank, and remains there till replaced by his Captain. [If Line is re-formed *on the March* from an Echellon formed to the *Left;*—Each Coverer, at the word FORWARD, makes way for his Captain (who will in that case change his flank) to move up on the right of his Company.]

FORM LINE ON THE LEADING COMPANY.

(*Suppose the ori-*

(B.) *Line oblique to the original Line.*

The Coverer of each Company that is wheeled forward or backward preparatory to the formation of the

ginal wheel was
4 paces.)
REMAINING
COMPANIES:
TWO PACES
ON THE —
BACKWARDS
WHEEL.

Q. MARCH.

FORM LINE:
Q. MARCH.

new Line, proceeds as directed for *the* 'remaining Coverers' in No. 19 (A), or No. 24.

The leading Company (or the remaining Companies) having been wheeled as may be necessary :‡ —The Coverer and Supernumerary Serjeant of the Company of formation will give the base points on its flanks; the Coverer furthest from the Captain, and both facing to the point of *appui*. [The inner *aide* will give a base point at arm's length from the Supernumerary Serjeant.]

On the 2nd word MARCH—The remaining Coverers march off on the outward flanks of their respective Companies : running out (as usual) to take up their covering in the line of Coverers.

‡ The Company of formation will be wheeled up from the original alignment at double the angle that the remainder are wheeled : or, the remainder will be wheeled to half the angle that the Company of formation is wheeled.

No. 26. *A Battalion in Line changing Front by (Oblique) Echellon.*

(F. E., pp. 193–199.)

Suppose the Movement to be performed (as will generally be the case) by the Company of formation being wheeled into the required alignment by its Captain, on the *Caution ;* and the remainder wheeled *on moveable pivots* by word of the Battalion Commander :—

(A.) *Changing front on a flank Company, (Suppose No. 1.): the remainder thrown forward.*

CHANGE FRONT ON THE RIGHT COMPANY, LEFT THROWN FORWARD.

REMAINING COMPANIES: ON THE MOVE, RIGHT WHEEL. Q. MARCH.

FORWARD.

On his Captain's word ' Right wheel'—The Coverer of the Company of formation moves to the spot where its reverse flank will rest, and the Supernumerary Serjeant of that Company gives the 2nd base point on the pivot flank: both facing to the point of formation.

Each of the remaining Coverers, on the word FORWARD, places himself on the outer flank of his Company: running out (as usual) when within 20 paces of the alignment, to take up his covering in the line of points.

(B.) *Changing front on a flank Company (Suppose No. 1.): the remainder thrown back.*

CHANGE FRONT ON THE RIGHT COMPANY, LEFT THROWN BACK.

REMAINING COMPANIES: RIGHT-ABOUT FACE.

ON THE MOVE, LEFT WHEEL. Q. MARCH.

FORWARD.

The Coverer and Supernumerary Serjeant of the Company of formation will give the base points as in (A.)

Each of the other Coverers will march (while in Echellon) on the outward flank of his Company; and will run out, as usual, to take up his covering in the Line: taking care to leave room for his Company to pass clear of him; and, when the Company has passed over the alignment, taking a pace to his front (without losing his covering) in order not to interfere with the pivot flank of the next Company.

(C.) *Changing front on a central Company, or the centre of the Battalion: one Wing advanced, the other retired.*

CHANGE FRONT ON THE CENTRE [or No.— COMPANY.]

LEFT (or

If the change of front is on the centre of a Company:— the Coverer and Supernumerary Serjeant of that

RIGHT) WING:
or
COMPANIES
ON THF LEFT
(*or* RIGHT):
RIGHT-ABOUT
FACE.

ON THE MOVE,
INWARDS
WHEEL.
Q. MARCH.

FORWARD.

Company will give the base points: the former on the wheeling-forward flank; the latter, on the flank that wheels back. [The centre *aide* will give his base point at arm's length from the Coverer.]

If the change of front is on the centre of the Battalion:—the Coverer of each of the 2 centre Companies will move to where its outer flank will rest; facing inwards. [The centre Serjeant moves out to give a centre point; the centre *aide* giving his base point at arm's length from him.]

The Coverers of the Companies which are faced-about, proceed as in (B): the remainder, as in (A).

When the above Movements are to be performed from the Halt, *on fixed pivots*:—The Coverer of the named Company (unless that Company is to wheel the *Quarter* circle, in which case he will mark its wheeling flank as usual) will be directed to take his paces from the 8th file, and will be halted, by the *Battalion Commander* from the point of *appui*. Each of the remaining Coverers, on the word WHEEL, will take the ordered number of paces from the 8th file of his Company, in the usual manner.

E

No. 27. *Re-forming Line from Direct Echellon.*

(F. E., pp. 200—203.)

(A.) *Line parallel to the original Line.*

RE-FORM LINE ON No.— COMPANY.

On *the Caution*—The Coverer and Supernumerary Serjeant of the named Company give the base points; facing to the point of *appui.*

[REMAINING COMPANIES: or COMPANIES IN FRONT: RIGHT-ABOUT FACE.]

[If the formation is on a central Company, the centre *aide* will be placed in front of that flank of the Company of formation which was the pivot in Echellon.]

Q, MARCH.

The remaining Coverers run out (as usual) to mark when the outward flanks of their Companies will rest in Line.

FORM LINE TO THE —.

(B.) *Line at right angles to the original Line.*

BY COMPANIES, RIGHT WHEEL.

During the wheel—Each Coverer changes his flank: and when Line is formed, proceeds as in **(A).**

FORWARD.

(C.) *Line oblique to the original Line.*

FORM OBLIQUE ECHELLON ON THE LEADING COMPANY.

The directing (*i.e.* the outward) flank of the leading Company will be taken as the first point in the intended Line. The new alignment will then be determined by the Coverer of the leading Company moving back, and covering in the direction required: at wheeling distance from the pivot flank of his Company.

REMAINING COMPANIES: RIGHT [or LEFT] HALF FACE.

Q MARCH.

The other Coverers:—

WHEEL BACK INTO LINE: Q. MARCH.

On the Caution—Run back, and mark the point on which the pivot flank of the Company next in rear of them will rest; taking wheeling distance, in succession, from base points. Having taken their distance and covering, they will face in the same direction as the leading Company.

When the Oblique Echellon that will then be formed is wheeled back into Line, each Coverer proceeds as in No. 25 (A).

SEC. VII.—SQUARES.

No. 28. *A Battalion in Column forming Square on any named Company.*

(F. E., p. 173.)

ON THE
LEADING
COMPANY,
FORM SQUARE.

Q. *(or* D.)
MARCH.

[When Square is formed from Open Column, the word SECTIONS OUTWARDS is given by the Battalion Commander : when from Quarter-distance Column, the Captains of central Companies give that word.]

(1) *Square on the leading Company.*

The Coverer of the leading Company will run to the rear of No. 2 on the Battalion Commander's word Q. MARCH, or on his Captain's word *Halt: dress,* according as the Column is halted or on the march.

The Coverers of the 2 rear Companies of the Column run into Square the moment the 3rd Company from the rear brings *Sections outwards.*

(2) *Square on the rear Company.*

ON THE REAR
COMPANY,
FORM SQUARE.

RIGHT-ABOUT
FACE.

Q. (or D.)
MARCH.

The Coverers of the rear, and rear-but-one, Companies will run round and place themselves close to the proper front rank of the latter, at the Battalion Commander's word Q. MARCH ; or (if the Column is on the march) when the Captain of the rear Company gives *Halt: dress.*

The Coverers of Nos. 1 and 2 will run into Square as No. 3 turns to the front preparatory to bringing *Sections outwards.*

(3) *Square on any central Company.*

(Suppose Right in front.)
ON THE LEFT-
CENTRE
COMPANY,
FORM SQUARE.

RIGHT-WING:
RIGHT-ABOUT
FACE.

Q. (or D.)
MARCH.

The Coverers of central Companies get into Square when the Companies in their present front bring *Sections outwards:* the remainder, as in (1) and (2).

No. 29. *A Battalion in Line forming Square on any named Company, and re-forming Line.*

(F. E., p. 180.)

(A.) *Forming Square.*

ON THE LEFT-
CENTRE
COMPANY,
FORM SQUARE.

FOURS
INWARDS.

Q. MARCH.

[This formation will usually be on the Left-centre Company.]

Coverers lead the front rank of their respective Companies (as usual) while in fours.

The Coverer of No. 1 should run on into Square before No. 2 brings *Sections outwards.*

(B.) *Re-forming Line.*

The Square will be formed into Column, and then deployed : Coverers proceeding as in No. 23.

No. 30. *A Battalion in Line forming Square Two-deep, and re-forming Line.*

(F. E., p. 184.)

(A.) *Forming Square.*

ON THE TWO CENTRE COMPANIES, TWO-DEEP: FORM SQUARE.

Q. MARCH.

On the word SQUARE—The Coverer of each of the 2 flank Companies (the Coverer of the right-flank Company changing flank) places himself in front of his leading file.

The Coverers of the right- and left-centre Companies (the former having first changed his flank) step back into Square.

Each of the remaining right-wing Coverers when his Captain changes his flank, places himself on the proper right of the proper rear rank of his Company. The remaining left-wing Coverers change flanks, and place themselves on the proper left of the proper rear rank of their respective Companies.

On the word MARCH—The Coverers of the Companies in Echellon march off on their outward flanks, till they run on to take up their distance in the Square.

(B.) *Re-forming Line.*

On the word LINE—The Coverer of each of the 2 flank Companies places himself in front of his leading file. The Coverers of the 2 centre Companies move out of Square, and mark the outward flanks of those Companies.

On the word MARCH—The Coverers of the 2 flank Companies lead straight out; those of the side-face Companies move up on their outward flanks while in Echellon: each Coverer running out, as usual, to take up his covering in the Line.

THE END.

FIG. I.

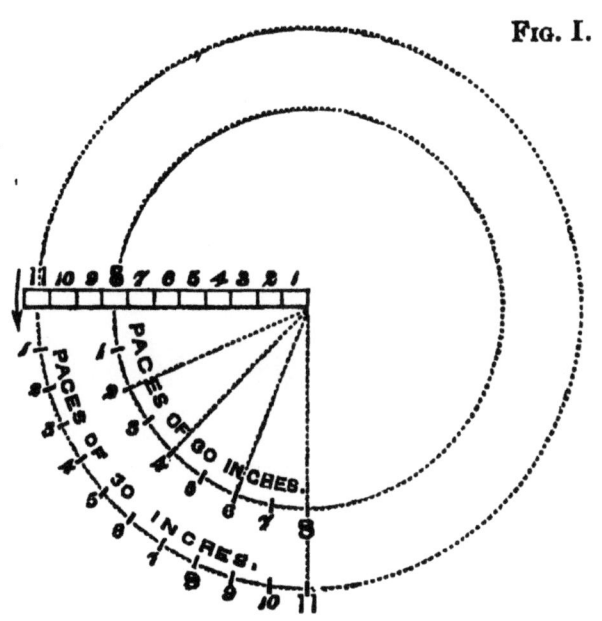

FIG. II.

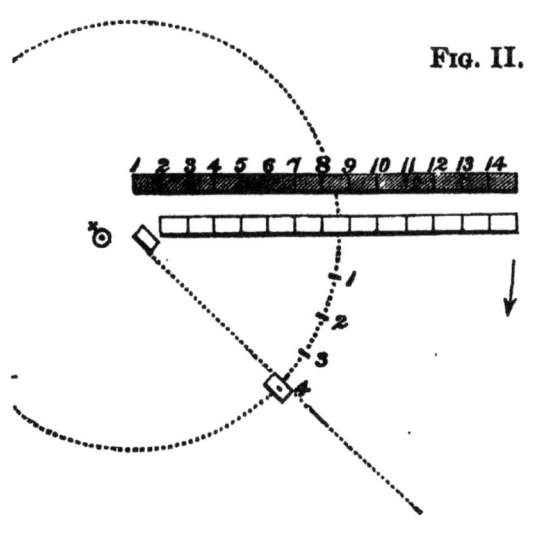